Dear Parent:
Your child's love of reading starts here!

Every child learns to read in a different way and at his or her own speed. Some go back and forth between reading levels and read favorite books again and again. Others read through each level in order. You can help your young reader improve and become more confident by encouraging his or her own interests and abilities. From books your child reads with you to the first books he or she reads alone, there are I Can Read Books for every stage of reading:

SHARED READING
Basic language, word repetition, and whimsical illustrations, ideal for sharing with your emergent reader

BEGINNING READING
Short sentences, familiar words, and simple concepts for children eager to read on their own

READING WITH HELP
Engaging stories, longer sentences, and language play for developing readers

READING ALONE
Complex plots, challenging vocabulary, and high-interest topics for the independent reader

ADVANCED READING
Short paragraphs, chapters, and exciting themes for the perfect bridge to chapter books

I Can Read Books have introduced children to the joy of reading since 1957. Featuring award-winning authors and illustrators and a fabulous cast of beloved characters, I Can Read Books set the standard for beginning readers.

A lifetime of discovery begins with the magical words **"I Can Read!"**

Visit www.icanread.com for information
on enriching your child's reading experience.

For Laura Parish Lake
and Herman Stanley Parish IV,
with love

Color markers and a black pen were used for the full-color art.

HarperCollins®, 🏠®, and I Can Read Book® are trademarks of HarperCollins Publishers.

Library of Congress Cataloging-in-Publication Data

Parish, Peggy.
  Merry Christmas, Amelia Bedelia / by Peggy Parish ; pictures by Lynn Sweat.
    p. cm. — (An I can read book)
  "Greenwillow Books."
  Summary: As Amelia Bedelia helps Mrs. Rogers prepare for Christmas, she bakes a date cake with a calendar in it and stuffs the children's stockings with turkey stuffing.
  ISBN-10: 0-688-06102-8 (lib. bdg.) — ISBN-13: 978-0-688-06102-9 (lib. bdg.)
  ISBN-10: 0-06-009945-3 (pbk.) — ISBN-13: 978-0-06-009945-9 (pbk.)
  [1. Christmas—Fiction. 2. Humorous stories.] I. Sweat, Lynn, ill. II. Title.
PZ7.P219Me 1986   85-24919
[E]   CIP
                                                     AC

17 SCP 20 19 18 17
❖ Originally published by Greenwillow Books, an imprint of HarperCollins Publishers, in 1986.

I Can Read!

2
READING
WITH HELP

Merry Christmas, Amelia Bedelia

story by Peggy Parish
pictures by Lynn Sweat

HarperCollins*Publishers*

"Amelia Bedelia," said Mrs. Rogers,

"Christmas is just around the corner."

"It is?" said Amelia Bedelia.

"Which corner?"

Mrs. Rogers laughed and said,

"I mean tomorrow is Christmas Day."

"I know that," said Amelia Bedelia.

"There's still so much to do,"

said Mrs. Rogers.

"We'll never finish!"

"We'll make it," said Amelia Bedelia.

"Just tell me what to do."

"First," said Mrs. Rogers,
"make a date cake.
Put lots of dates in it."
"All right," said Amelia Bedelia.
She started to the kitchen.

"Wait," said Mrs. Rogers.

"Put these nuts in the cake, too."

She gave Amelia Bedelia

a bag of nuts.

"Anything else?" said Amelia Bedelia.

"Do pop some corn," said Mrs. Rogers.

"I want to make popcorn balls."

"How much should I pop?"

said Amelia Bedelia.

"I'll need six cups," said Mrs. Rogers.

Amelia Bedelia went to the kitchen.
"I have never heard of date cake,"
she said.
"But I'll try my hand at it."

Amelia Bedelia put some of this
and a little of that into a bowl.
She mixed and she mixed.
Soon her batter was ready.

"Now," she said,

"I need lots of dates."

Amelia Bedelia thought about this.

"A calendar!" she said.

"That has lots of dates."

Amelia Bedelia got a calendar.

She cut off all of the dates.

She dumped them into the cake.

"Now for the nuts,"

said Amelia Bedelia.

She opened the bag of nuts.

She dumped them into the cake.

Amelia Bedelia mixed some more.

Then she put the cake

in the oven.

"I'll make a spice cake, too,"

she said.

"I do love spice cake."

So Amelia Bedelia

made a spice cake.

"Now for the popcorn," she said.

Amelia Bedelia measured

six cups of corn.

Then she popped and she popped

and she popped.

"Mrs. Rogers must love

popcorn balls,"

said Amelia Bedelia.

Amy came to the back door.

"Amelia Bedelia," she called.

"Santa Claus is coming tonight."

"He's coming here?"

said Amelia Bedelia.

"Yes," said Amy.

"Thank you for telling me,"
said Amelia Bedelia.
"I'll tell Mrs. Rogers."
Amy went on her way.

"That cake smells good,"

said Mrs. Rogers.

She came into the kitchen.

She stopped.

"Amelia Bedelia!" she said.

"Why did you pop so much corn?

I only need six cups."

"And I popped six cups,"

said Amelia Bedelia.

"I meant six cups of popped corn,"

said Mrs. Rogers.

"Then you should have said so,"
said Amelia Bedelia.
"I know," said Mrs. Rogers.

"Amy said Santa Claus
is coming tonight,"
said Amelia Bedelia.
"Did you know that?"
"Oh yes!" said Mrs. Rogers.
"He comes every year.
Don't you remember him?"

"You mean the man
in the red suit?"
said Amelia Bedelia.
"The one who
comes down chimneys?"

"That's right," said Mrs. Rogers.

"Oh my," said Amelia Bedelia.

"That chimney is a sight.

I'll have to clean it."

Mrs. Rogers laughed and said,

"Don't bother. Santa Claus

will manage."

The telephone rang.

"I'll get it," said Mrs. Rogers.

"I'll see to my cakes,"

said Amelia Bedelia.

She opened the oven.

"Just right," she said.

"I'll set them out to cool."

"Oh, Amelia Bedelia,"

called Mrs. Rogers.

"This is dreadful."

Amelia Bedelia ran to Mrs. Rogers.

"What is it?" she said.

"We forgot

about Aunt Myra.

We must go

and get her,"

said Mrs. Rogers.

"Can you finish everything?"

said Mrs. Rogers.

"Of course I can,"

said Amelia Bedelia.

"I made a list," said Mrs. Rogers.

"I hope you will understand it."

"Don't you worry,"

said Amelia Bedelia.

"We will be back about eight o'clock,"
said Mrs. Rogers.

"Aunt Myra loves Christmas carols.
Could you greet her with some?"

"I'll do my best," said Amelia Bedelia.

A car horn blew.

"That's Mr. Rogers,"

said Mrs. Rogers.

She went out to the car.

"I better get busy,"

said Amelia Bedelia.

"What must I do first?"

She looked at the list and read,

"Stuff six stockings

for the neighbors' children."

Amelia Bedelia shook her head.

"Now that beats all,"

she said.

"I've stuffed turkeys.

But I've never

stuffed stockings."

30

Amelia Bedelia went to the kitchen.

"That will take lots of stuffing,"

she said.

So she made pans and pans of it.

"That should do it,"

said Amelia Bedelia.

She found six stockings.

And Amelia Bedelia stuffed them.

She looked at her list.

"Hang the stockings on the mantel."

Amelia Bedelia got some rope.

She hung those stockings

on the mantel.

"Stuffed and hung," she said.

"What's next? Trim the tree."

Amelia Bedelia looked

at the tree.

"It looks fine to me," she said.

"But if she wants it trimmed,

I'll trim it."

So Amelia Bedelia

trimmed the tree.

"Maybe it was too fat," she said.

Amelia Bedelia looked at the list.

"Oh, oh," she said.

"I have to go to the store."

In a bit Amelia Bedelia was back.
"The list says to put on
colored balls," she said.
"I hope I bought enough."

Amelia Bedelia put colored balls

on the tree.

But the balls rolled right off.

"Shoot!" she said.

"I'm going to tie you on."

And she did.

"String on lots of lights,"

read Amelia Bedelia.

She found lots of lights.

She found some string.

And she strung on those lights.

"What a fancy tree,"

said Amelia Bedelia.

"I wonder what's next?"

She looked at the list.

"My word," she said.

"Put a big star on top of the tree.

What kind of star does she want?

A movie star? A rock star?

A baseball star?"

Amelia Bedelia sat down to think.
"I would like to be a star,"
she said.
"I guess everybody would."
Suddenly Amelia Bedelia
had an idea.
"That's it," she said.

"Everybody can be a star

on this tree."

Amelia Bedelia made a sign.

It said,

She put it on the tree.

She got a mirror.

She tied it on the top

of the tree.

Amelia Bedelia looked

in the mirror.

"Hurray!" she said. "I'm a star."

Amelia Bedelia looked at the list.

"That's it," she said.

"I'll make those popcorn balls.

Mrs. Rogers won't have time."

Amelia Bedelia made dozens

of popcorn balls.

"Maybe Mrs. Rogers wanted these
for the tree," she said.
"I'll put them on."
Amelia Bedelia wrapped the balls.
She tied them on the tree.
"That does look nice," she said.
"Now I must make
some telephone calls."

Amelia Bedelia made her calls.

She looked at the clock.

"My, it's getting late," she said.

"I need some supper."

Amelia Bedelia made her supper.

She ate it.

Then she cleaned up the kitchen.

"The folks will be here soon,"

she said.

"I'll wait up front for them."

A little later the doorbell rang.

Amelia Bedelia opened the door.

"Come in," she said.

Three children came in.

They sat and talked

with Amelia Bedelia.

A car turned into the drive.

"Here they are," said Amelia Bedelia.

"You know what to do."

The door opened.

"We're here," said Mrs. Rogers.

Aunt Myra came in.

"Now!" said Amelia Bedelia.

"Greetings, greetings, greetings,"
said the three children.
"What's this about?"
said Mrs. Rogers.
"You said to greet Aunt Myra
with Carols," said Amelia Bedelia.
"Here's Carol Lee,
Carol Green,
and Carol Lake."

"What lovely Carols,"
said Aunt Myra.
"Thank you."
The children left.

Mrs. Rogers saw the tree.

"Amelia Bedelia!" she shouted.

"What did you do to that tree?"

"Popcorn balls!" shouted Aunt Myra.

"I love popcorn balls."

She ran to the tree.

"Look!" shouted Aunt Myra.

"I'm a star!"

Mrs. Rogers began to splutter.

"Don't be angry, dear,"

said Mr. Rogers. "It's Christmas.

And Aunt Myra is happy.

Be thankful for that!"

"Oh, all right," said Mrs. Rogers.

"Let's have some cake."

"Just what I wanted," said Mr. Rogers.

They all went to the kitchen.

"Amelia Bedelia," said Mrs. Rogers,

"where is my cake?"

Amelia Bedelia put the cake

on the table.

Mr. Rogers sliced it.

"What kind of cake is this?" he said.

"It's full of paper and rocks."

"Let me see the paper,"

said Aunt Myra.

She looked at it.

"I know!" she said.

"It's a date cake."

"And your rocks are nuts,"
said Amelia Bedelia.

"So they are," said Mr. Rogers.

"I was all set for some good cake."

"Here you are," said Amelia Bedelia.

She gave him her cake.

"Spice cake!" said Aunt Myra.

"Amelia Bedelia, you're my kind
of person."

"Delicious," said Mr. Rogers.

"I'll have another piece,"

said Mrs. Rogers.

"So will I," said Aunt Myra.

They ate until most of the cake

was gone.

"It's past my bedtime," said Aunt Myra.
"We should all go to sleep,"
said Mrs. Rogers.
"You, too, Amelia Bedelia,"
said Mr. Rogers. "Santa Claus
won't come if you're awake."
"He can wait a bit," said Amelia Bedelia.
"I have work to do."

Amelia Bedelia washed the dishes.

She heard something outside.

"What is that?" she said.

Amelia Bedelia opened the door.

"Santa Claus!" she said.

"Wait till I tell the folks!"

"Shhhh," said Santa Claus.

"You should be asleep.

You shouldn't see me."

Amelia Bedelia closed her eyes.

"Now I can't see you," she said.

"Please go to bed," said Santa Claus.

"I have work to do."

"I'm on my way," said Amelia Bedelia.

"Good night, Santa Claus,"
called Amelia Bedelia.
"Good night," called Santa Claus.
"And Merry Christmas,
Amelia Bedelia."